DOMINIQUE MOCEANU

AN AMERICAN CHAMPION

DOMINIQUE MOCEANU

AN AMERICAN CHAMPION

AN AUTOBIOGRAPHY

AS TOLD TO STEVE WOODWARD

A Yearling Book

Published by
Bantam Doubleday Dell Books for Young Readers
a division of
Bantam Doubleday Dell Publishing Group, Inc.
1540 Broadway
New York, New York 10036

ISBN: 0-440-41433-4

Reprinted by arrangement with Bantam Books for Young Readers
Printed in the United States of America
October 1997
10 9 8 7 6 5 4 3 2 1
CWO

CONTENTS

INTRODUCTION BY BELA KAROLYI — viii

MY JOURNEY — ix

PROLOGUE: FOUR MAGIC WORDS — 1

1. I Think She Has It — 5

2. LaFleur's Gymnastics — 8

3. Big Changes — 11

4. Starting at Bela's — 17

5. Finding My Bearings — 22

6. Preparing for the Nationals — 26

7. Stress Busters — 33

8. My Training Schedule — 36

9. Competitive Savvy — 45

10. The Vault — 50

11. The Uneven Parallel Bars — 55

12. The Balance Beam — 59

13. The Floor Exercise — 63

14. Fame and Fans — 68

15. My Normal Life   77

16. Downtime   81

17. I'm a Fan Too   85

18. On the Go   87

19. Countdown to the Olympics   93

AFTERWORD   99

A FEW OF MY FAVORITE THINGS   100

GUIDE TO GYMNASTIC EVENTS AND
    SCORING   102

BASIC GYMNASTIC MOVES AND
    POSITIONS   111

*With love and thanks to Mom, Dad,
and my little sister, Christina.*

*And to Bela and Marta Karolyi and
Geza Pozsar for all their help in making
my dream come true.*
—D.M.

Introduction by
Bela Karolyi

Wow! That's what I say every time I see Dominique Moceanu whip through her floor exercise and balance beam routines. She just sparkles! Seeing a young gymnast I've coached catapult to the top of the sport, especially someone with her crowd-winning smile, dynamism, drive, and phenomenal talent, gives me great pride. Dominique loves gymnastics, and it shows! She is a true competitor—just the way my former pupils and Olympic gold medalists Mary Lou Retton and Nadia Comaneci were. Dominique is a gymnast who goes out and gives a hundred and ten percent of herself in every routine she executes. She deserves to be our national champion and the hope of our American team to medal at the 1996 Summer Olympics in Atlanta. I am rooting for her every step of the way.

Dominique is an American champion—and an inspiration to all Olympic athletes.

MY JOURNEY

1979 My father, Dimitry Moceanu, leaves his native Romania to begin a new life in the United States. My mother, Camelia, joins him in early 1981.

1981 My birthday: September 30 in Hollywood, California.

1983 My family moves to Highland Park, Illinois, near Chicago, where I see snow for the first time. Later, between my third and fourth birthdays, my parents enroll me in gymnastics classes at a nearby club.

1985 After I get my first passport, my parents whisk me off for a forty-five-day European vacation.

My father contacts fellow native Romanian Bela Karolyi at Karolyi's now-famous gymnastics training center in Houston. He inquires about enrolling me in the school. Bela Karolyi urges him to wait until I reach age nine or ten.

1987 My family moves to Tampa, Florida. I enroll at LaFleur's Gymnastics, where I continue to advance.

  August 24. My sister, Christina, is born.

  After my tenth birthday, my family moves to Houston. I have told my father my wish to train at Karolyi's. His reply: "Okay. We will go!" On December 18, I arrive for the first session.

1992 United States National Championships, Junior Division
Silver: Balance Beam
Only seven months after joining Karolyi's, I medal in the junior Nationals—the youngest junior qualifier ever to do so (age ten). I finish fifth all-around.

 1993 United States National Championships, Junior Division
This is one of my greatest competitions, even though I mess up on a couple of things. I finish seventh all-around.

 1994 United States National Championships, Junior Division
Gold Medal: All-Around; Gold Medal: Floor Exercise; Gold Medal: Vault; Bronze Medal: Balance Beam; Bronze Medal: Uneven Bars
I am thrilled to win my very first all-around title.

 1995 Reese's International Gymnastics Cup
Gold Medal: Uneven Bars; Bronze Medal: Balance Beam
A good meet.

 1995 American Classic
Gold Medal: Vault; Silver Medal Tie: All-Around; Bronze Medal: Balance Beam; Bronze Medal: Floor Exercise
An even better meet.

1995 VISA Challenge, Senior Division
Gold Medal: All-Around; Gold Medal: Floor Exercise; Gold Medal: Team Competition; Silver Medal: Uneven Bars; Bronze Medal: Balance Beam; Bronze Medal: Vault
Not only is this my first all-around title against an international field, but I also medal big-time in numerous events. It is a great meet. Meng Fei of China trails me.

1995 **United States National Championships, Senior Division**
Gold Medal: All-Around; Silver Medal: Floor Exercise;
Bronze Medal: Vault
*At thirteen, I become the youngest gymnast in U.S. history to
capture the all-around title.*

1995 **World Team Trials**
Gold Medal: All-Around
*As at the National Championships, I finish first, Shannon
Miller second, Jaycie Phelps third.*

1995 **World Championships (Sabae, Japan), Senior Division**
Silver Medal: Balance Beam; Bronze Medal: Team Competition
*Even though I do not win as many medals as I'd hoped, I see
that my routines can compete against those of the top gymnasts.
Summer Olympics, here I come! (I finish fifth all-around, the
best finish for an American.)*

Prologue:
Four Magic Words

I remember that day so clearly, as if it were a movie that I can replay in my mind. I had just turned ten years old. My family and I were living in Tampa, Florida, where my father, Dimitry, owned a car dealership and my mother, Camelia, was a hair-stylist. Although it was October, it was still very warm outside, thanks to Florida's tropical climate.

That Saturday afternoon, I was parked in front of the television, watching my favorite sport: gymnastics. I had been studying gymnastics myself since I was three years old, and I loved watching my idols perform on television. I already knew all the major gymnasts' names, their coaches' names, the names of their gyms—anything I could find out about them. I was obsessed.

"Go, Betty!" I shouted. "Nail it! Nail the landing!" Betty Okino, one of the top five gymnasts in the country in 1991, performed a Yurchenko vault with a double twist, and stuck her dismount.

"All right!" I punched the air, excited at seeing her do so well. Betty Okino, Kim Zmeskal, and Kerri Strug were the reigning female gymnasts at the time. Whenever they were on television, I was there, my nose glued to the screen. These were athletes I looked up to and respected. They were the best. I wanted to be just like them.

But they all lived in Houston, Texas, where they were coached by Bela Karolyi, the most famous gymnastics coach in the entire world. I lived in Tampa, where I attended LaFleur's Gymnastics. I loved my teachers, Jeff LaFleur and Beth Hair, but I knew it wasn't the same as being coached by Bela.

Bela had turned out one champion after another—more than any other coach. Nadia Comaneci, Mary Lou Retton, Kim, Betty, and Kerri—all were his students.

"Oh, if only I could train with Bela," I moaned softly to myself, watching the television. "I want to be like Kim and Nadia." I sighed. "Someday I will," I promised myself.

Suddenly a voice spoke behind me, saying four words that would change my life—that are still changing my life.

"Okay," my father said. "We will go."

"What?" I turned and smiled at him. I hadn't even known he was in the room. "Go where?"

"We will go to Houston," Dad continued. "We will move there—all of us—so you can go to Karolyi's every day and train. That's what your mother and I have decided to do."

I just stared at him. "But—but—" I sputtered.

My father shook his head and smiled. "No buts."

And that's how we suddenly moved to Houston when I was ten. That's how I came to Bela's.

1

I THINK
SHE HAS IT

It might sound as if my gymnastics career began when I finally started training with Bela Karolyi. But actually it began before I was even born!

In their home country of Romania, both of my parents were gymnasts. Dad competed with the junior national team, and Mom was enrolled in youth gymnastics programs. When they married, they promised each other their first child would be a gymnast or some other kind of athlete. My dad says he wanted his children to have the discipline and determination that an athlete develops. After all, he figured, discipline and the ability to work hard toward a goal were good qualities that would be useful no matter what you decided to do with your life.

In 1979, soon after their marriage, my father left

Romania and came to America, where he felt he could make a better life for himself and his family. A year later, my mother followed him to California. I was born in Hollywood, California, on September 30, 1981. So I am American!

Because my parents are Romanian, and because people think I resemble a famous Romanian gymnast, Nadia Comaneci, many people assume that I am Romanian too. But I feel very American. I've always lived in America, most of my friends are American, and I go to American schools.

I am very lucky, though: At home, my parents, my little sister, Christina, and I all speak Romanian. So I am bilingual. It helps my parents preserve their heritage. They want Christina and me to be proud of being American but not to forget our ancestral ties to the homeland. I feel as if I have the best of both worlds: I enjoy the freedom of our American lifestyle (not to mention American clothes, music, and television), plus I have the added richness of a Romanian background, through both the language and my mother's fabulous Romanian cooking. It's a great combination.

Anyway, it wasn't long after I was born that my parents began watching me for signs that I might be a good gymnast someday. When I was only six months old, my dad even gave me the ultimate test.

He strung a clothesline in our kitchen.

"Let's see how strong Domi is," Dad said. Carefully he held me up to the clothesline, and I wrapped my hands around it. I don't remember doing this, but he said I was laughing, as if I thought it was a game.

My mother stood right next to me, her hands outstretched, in case I needed her to catch me.

Then Dad slowly let go of me, so that I was hanging on the clothesline. They waited and waited for my grip to weaken, but I hung on. I guess I was stubborn! As the minutes passed, my parents looked at each other with pride and excitement.

"I think she has it, Camelia," my father told my mother. "I think she will go all the way."

My mother nodded happily in agreement. Later they told me that the clothesline actually broke before I would let go! And that was my first gymnastics test. I'm glad I passed it, and I'm glad my parents saw so much potential in me even back then.

2

LAFLEUR'S
GYMNASTICS

After I passed the clothesline test, my father called Bela Karolyi at his gym in Houston. Coincidentally, Bela had emigrated to the United States at about the same time my parents had, and he had also begun his new life in California. Then he had settled in Texas and founded his gymnastics training camp.

When my father called Bela, he explained that I was only three but that I seemed born to be a gymnast. My father knew all about Bela, and about the new star he was training, Mary Lou Retton.

Bela seemed impressed with my father's faith in me but replied that I was still too young for formal training. He advised my dad to enroll me in a local gymnastics club. "If she is still progressing around the age of nine," Bela told my father, "call me again and we will talk. Then maybe the time will be right. Be patient."

By that point, we had moved from California to Highland Park, Illinois, where my parents enrolled me in my first gymnastics classes. But two years later, in 1985, we landed in Tampa. It was in Tampa that my parents enrolled me at LaFleur's Gymnastics.

My parents tell me now that during those years, between 1985 and 1991, they were just biding their time. Even back then, they had faith that someday I would be coached by Bela, and that I would be a great gymnast.

But for now I was just a little kid, taking gymnastics classes, attending school, making friends. In some ways I had a totally normal life, but I had already been bitten by the gymnastics bug. I loved gymnastics more than anything. I always have, for as long as I can remember.

All I wanted to do all day was hang out at LaFleur's and play, play, play. I loved learning new skills, but I also just liked having fun. If I messed up, it was no big deal. My mom was always there telling me everything was all right, whether it was or not. To me it was the most fun thing in the whole world.

The owner and head coach, Jeff LaFleur, became a friend of my family's. I really adored him and Beth Hair, who was the balance beam coach. They're really nice people. I loved LaFleur's so much that I always stayed after my regular class—especially when they had "open gym" on Friday nights. My friends and I would hang out, trying new skills, running all over the place, pretending we were famous gymnasts. Back then I didn't take gymnastics as seriously as I do now. It was more like recreation.

When I was seven, I went to my very first competition—a small local event. Of course, I had no idea what competing meant or how it was different from training or practicing. I just showed up at the gym, waited my turn, watched the other gymnasts, and then did my routine. I didn't even care about doing well, or where I ranked in relation to other gymnasts.

Then I did my skills. And people applauded. They applauded for *me*. Everyone in the audience was cheering for *me*. I looked over and saw my parents smiling and waving. I think that's when I knew I was really hooked—there was no turning back. I liked being in the limelight. All of a sudden I wished I had done better. I resolved right then to compete again, and to do my absolute best, from then on.

3

BIG CHANGES

After that first competition, I started working in earnest. My parents and my teachers noticed a change in me. I was still playing a lot at the gym and having a good time, but I was also more serious. I wanted to learn new skills and get better at everything. Sometimes I was even in too much of a hurry to learn new things—I didn't always perfect what I already knew.

"Slow down," my coach told me. "Take your time. You must learn step A before you go on to step B."

It wasn't until later that I truly understood that lesson.

My body was growing, getting older, and almost overnight it felt as if I had a whole new me to get used to. When I was younger I hadn't cared about competition. But when I was eight and nine I cared much more. Then when I messed up, it really set off my temper. I *knew* I could do better. I knew I had to.

I competed more often. In the beginning, I never did well at a competition. I would catch a glimpse of my mother out of the corner of my eye, and it would make me terribly nervous.

I knew what I had to do, what I *wanted* to do, but somehow it just didn't happen for me. When I was first starting as a competitor, I made mistakes at every single meet. I remember thinking, "Why can't I do this stuff?" I had no patience for failure or mistakes. Now I realize that there was no way I could be perfect when I was so young. And I also realize that if my mistakes hadn't bothered me so much then, I might not have gotten as far as I have today.

Even though I disappointed myself when I competed, I still loved everything about gymnastics. To me, a perfect day was when I could get up, eat breakfast, and spend all day at the gym. That was when I started to learn about making choices.

To be the best at anything, even to be really good at anything, you have to devote a lot of time and effort and energy to it. You have to do this *one* thing at the expense of other things you might enjoy. Sometimes I had to choose between going to the gym to practice and going to the mall with my friends, or watching television, or riding my bike, or playing with my baby sister, Christina, who was born when I was eight. I had to choose. Ninety-nine percent of the time, I chose gymnastics. There was no contest. I was lucky: I knew what I wanted to do. Some people go through their whole life and never know. But I did.

And my parents were the best. They supported me strongly and encouraged me every way they could. They always showed me their love, and that helped me continue. We discussed everything, good and bad, and they advised me. Remember, they had been gymnasts themselves. So their insights were very helpful to me. We still have that relationship today. I wouldn't change it for anything.

Finally, without my knowing, Dad called Bela again. He told Bela that I still showed exceptional promise. He said we wanted to come to Houston so that I could train with Bela.

Bela said, "All right." I guess he knew my dad meant business!

Until the moment when my father said, "Okay.

We will go," training at Karolyi's had been only a dream for me. Even though I wished I could train there, I felt lucky to have as much as I did. My parents supported me and bought me leotards and drove me back and forth to class at LaFleur's, where my coaches were so great to me. . . . I had a nice life in a nice house in a nice town. I didn't know that my parents were planning to give me more.

Just a few short weeks after my father uttered those four magic words, we had packed up everything from our house in Tampa and were on the road to Houston. I knew only three things about our new state, Texas: Houston was there, Bela Karolyi was there, and I'd heard a television announcer say that Mary Lou Retton still lived there.

When we left Tampa, I was almost ten, and my sister was almost two. I remember feeling excited beyond belief, as if I were in a dream. Training with Bela had been my fondest wish, and now it was all coming true. Sometimes I worried that I would wake up from this wonderful fantasy to find that it was all in my imagination. But it wasn't.

It's a good thing I was only ten years old—if I had been any older, I might have been scared to death at all the changes. A new state, new city, new house, new jobs for my parents—it was all happening because of me, only me. Just so that I, Dominique Moceanu, would have the chance to train under the world's most famous gymnastics coach.

But my parents were amazing. They never let me feel any of that pressure. They made it sound as if it was the best thing for us as a family. I wanted to be a fantastic gymnast, and they wanted that for me too. So in their minds, the move made sense.

My mother left her job in a hair salon. My father was reluctant to lose his car dealership in Tampa, so for the first eighteen months he commuted between Houston and Tampa. My mother, sister, grandparents, and I lived in a rented house in Houston. Dad would come to stay with us on the weekends.

We eventually got very tired of being apart all the time. It was so hard when Monday came and we had to say good-bye. Finally, in 1993, Dad sold his car dealership and moved to Houston for good. I was really happy about it, and so were the rest of my family. Dad took a job at a Ford dealership here in town. He's very good at his job and soon became sales manager. Within a short while, he was back to running his own dealership, specializing in the sale of imported cars. I'm very proud of his determination and hard work. In his life, he's had to start over many times, and each time he makes the best of his situation. That's a real inspiration to me.

4

STARTING AT BELA'S

When I first walked into Karolyi's Gymnastics, in December 1991, I was battling nerves and fear. Have you heard that old saying "Be careful what you wish for—you might get it"? That's how I felt. I didn't know where to go, what to do, how to act. I wasn't sure if I was even good enough to stay there and train. For years I had dreamed of and wished for the chance to work with Bela Karolyi. Now my dream had come true, and it suddenly felt like a nightmare. Was I good enough? I would find out.

When I first came to Karolyi's Gymnastics, the blue gym was still being built. Today Bela's training center is made up of three gyms, covering 28,000 square feet. Two of the gyms are for younger gymnasts, and one gym is for the elite gymnasts only—such as Betty Okino, Kerri Strug, and Kim Zmeskal. The elite gym has pale blue walls. The other two have tan walls. Everyone who comes to Bela's to train hopes one day to make it to the blue gym. Each new gymnast looks at the blue gym and dreams of the day when she might be back there, preparing for a major championship, with Bela and his wife, Marta, watching over every skill. I started at one of the tan gyms, along with dozens of other girls from different age groups.

When I first met Bela, I was totally intimidated by him. Not many people get to meet him, and I was so nervous about it that my stomach hurt. He's a big guy, with a big mustache. He dashes around so that it seems as if he's everywhere at once. I felt as if I came up only to his kneecaps!

On top of meeting Bela, guess who worked out every day in the same gym I did—Kim Zmeskal, Kerri Strug, and Betty Okino! I was so in awe of them. They had been my heroes for years, and here they were in person! I got to see firsthand how amazing they were, and how dedicated. I also saw, to my amazement, that they were human. They were just girls, like me. They had good days and bad days—

and great days. And they were so nice and helpful to me, right from the very beginning.

One of the first things that happened when I began training at Karolyi's was that I had to show Bela, Marta, and their choreographer, Geza Pozsar, my skills. (Geza is also from Romania and is now the national director of choreography for USA Gymnastics.) I had been one of the best gymnasts at my old gym, and now I performed all the skills I knew. But I was so nervous that I couldn't perform well. Bela thought my skills were sloppy. I knew how to do many things, but I did nothing perfectly. And perfection was what Bela wanted to see.

I had a lot to learn.

Marta Karolyi is a major part of the training program, even though Bela receives more publicity. That's fine with her. She prefers to let Bela be the face and the voice of the gym. But the two of them are a great team. In some ways they are very much alike—very determined and intense as they go about their work. They are like two lions pacing around the gym, seeing and understanding all. At first I found it terrifying, intimidating. Then I grew to see it as very comforting. I know they are always looking out for me, helping me do my best. Together they are one hundred percent focused on helping each one of their students be a little better than she was yesterday. Sometimes I still can't believe that I'm lucky enough to spend almost every day in their presence, growing and maturing as an athlete and as a person. It's a great feeling.

I also find their personal stories very inspiring. Back around 1981, the same year I was born, Bela, Marta, and Geza Pozsar toured the United States with the Romanian gymnastics team. Nadia Comaneci was their star—she was incredibly popular around the world. By 1981 she had completed two Olympic Games (the 1976 Games in Montreal and the 1980 Games in Moscow). The summer before this tour, Nadia had won Olympic gold medals in the floor exercise and beam, and a silver medal in the all-around competition.

When the tour ended in New York City, it was time for the Romanian visitors to return home. But by then, Bela, Marta, and Geza had become very frustrated with the Romanian government. Almost single-handedly, they had brought tremendous success to the Romanian gymnastics programs, but the government still treated them badly. So that last morning of the tour, the three of them just walked out of their hotel with a very small amount of luggage. They asked the American government for asylum, and America granted it. Just like my parents, the Karolyis and Geza created new lives for themselves from scratch. By working extremely hard, they overcame early difficulties to achieve their current well-deserved success.

So when my coaches say that nothing ever comes easy, I understand that no one knows it better than they do.

5

FINDING MY
BEARINGS

I quickly settled into a routine at my new gym.
Every day I woke up early and ate breakfast. One
of my parents would drive me to Karolyi's Gymnastics. There I worked hard with the other gymnasts
until midmorning. From eleven to three I attended
private school. Then it was back to the gym for
more practice. I would get home around eight
o'clock in the evening, eat dinner, do my schoolwork, maybe watch a little television, and then go
to bed.

Slowly I began to relearn all the lessons I had
rushed through back in Tampa. I had to *un*learn
many bad habits and replace them with correct
ones. I came to see that a big, flashy move meant
nothing if all my little moves were sloppy. As time

went on, my coaches taught me that every single gesture, every breath, every movement had to be precise and consistent and perfect, or the whole performance would fall apart. I guess I just had to mature some more, grow up a little.

In the early days I didn't study much with Bela and Marta. They focus their energies on their most elite gymnasts. But I remember one of my early experiences with them. (Bela still teases me about this.)

One day Geza Pozsar came into the gym to help me develop a new floor routine, one I could use while I sharpened my skills. Geza wanted to create a new program for me set to Hungarian music, starting off with a traditional step dance. The floor exercise used to be a nightmare for me, when I first came to Karolyi's. I had gotten into so many bad habits, I'm sure I just looked like a mess out there on the floor. For this new routine I was supposed to dance in a circle, counting off the steps, one, two, three, four, five, six, seven, eight . . . and then jump into a little pose. *Not* a difficult program. *Anyone* could do this. Anyone except me, as it turned out. No matter how I tried, I couldn't get the eight steps just right, and I couldn't figure out how to do the pose the right way. Geza spent an hour with me, trying to help me master this very simple beginning. By the end of the hour, I felt as if I couldn't even *count* to eight, much less dance in little steps.

Kim Zmeskal and Betty Okino, who were both training for the 1992 Summer Olympics, tried to help me as well. They counted the steps out loud and demonstrated the little pose. Of course they both did it perfectly the first time. I was so humiliated! Nothing helped. I felt so bad—I was really upset.

I think finally Geza just gave up and found something else that I *could* do. That was another important lesson for me: Sometimes you just have to try something new, even if you're worried about looking stupid. Sometimes you have to experiment with new moves. That's what training is all about, it's why you go to the gym . . . to explore possibilities.

Of course, Kim and Betty still laugh about how funny I was that day, how totally lame I looked. I just say, "Yeah, thanks. You don't have to remind me!"

Here's another big truth about gymnastics training: If you feel fear, you will not be able to achieve your best. It took me a while, but with everyone's patient help, I gradually overcame my fears. After only seven months with Bela, I made the Junior National team. That did a lot for my confidence. I was the youngest person ever to make the juniors. I guess Bela decided he was not sorry to have kept me!

In 1994 I won the All-Around Junior Champion award at the U.S. National Championships. And I received two gold medals—one for the vault, and one for the floor exercise. (Which I used to hate!) I also received bronze medals for the uneven parallel bars and the balance beam. I was so incredibly proud that day. I think those medals helped me feel that my parents' faith in me hadn't been misplaced. It made me much more confident. All along, I had hoped I could do it—now I really believed I could.

Finally, finally, I was able to let go of my last fears and to put myself totally into Bela's and Marta's hands. A real bond formed between me and the Karolyis—I could talk to them, share my hopes and dreams. I felt as if I belonged, as if I was part of the team, and I trusted them completely. And you know what? I blossomed even more as an athlete. By 1994 everyone at Karolyi's was not only part of my team, they were part of my family. And in that nurturing environment, I suddenly started to do better than I ever had before.

6

PREPARING FOR THE NATIONALS

In the early part of 1995, I trained out at Bela's ranch while the new blue gym was being constructed at the training center. The ranch, an hour outside Houston, is where he and Marta actually live. (It only *looks* as if he lives at the gym!) Bela's summer training camps are held at the ranch as well.

I love the ranch. The Karolyis keep horses, cows, pigs, even some llamas and a camel! Bela looks after all the animals himself. It's amazing to me that with all he has to do, he still has time to worry about everyone and everything around him. He has great strength of character—he always tries his best not to let things get to him. He has enormous will, and he's tough. When he tells his gymnasts how hard we have to work, we don't doubt him. We see how hard he pushes himself. Bela will not sit down, morning or night. He gets up at the crack of dawn and just keeps going. Few people can keep up with him.

In the first half of 1995, I did a couple of competitions. Each one was a thrill to be in, but I have to confess I looked upon them as warm-ups for the U.S. National Championships. They were good opportunities for me to work on what might be my greatest weakness: consistency in performance.

At the Reese's International Gymnastics Cup, I received a gold medal for the uneven bars, a bronze medal for the balance beam, and fourth place for the floor exercise.

At the American Classic, I won the gold medal for the vault, a silver medal for all-around, and two bronze medals—for the beam and the floor exercise.

The VISA Challenge was a terrific meet for me. I received my first gold medal as all-around champion in the senior division, and a gold for the floor exercise. I got a silver medal for the uneven bars, and two bronzes, for the beam and the vault. Plus, my team got a gold medal in the team competition. After that meet, I wasn't sure I could ever do better. For just a moment I forgot Karolyi's Law: You can always do better.

As soon as those meets were behind me, I began training in earnest for the Nationals, which were being held in New Orleans, Louisiana. There would be no interruptions, no other competitions until August.

Beginning in May, Geza and I put together the routines I would need, keeping in mind what degrees of difficulty were necessary to contend for a national championship.

In women's competition, a gymnast starts each event with a base score of 9.4. If you make a mistake, the judges will deduct fractions of a point. To bring your score closer to a perfect 10.0, you need to receive bonus points from the judges. These bonus points are given in fractions of a point also, such as one-tenth, two-tenths, etc. To compete at the elite level, there must be several moves that are rated very difficult—"E" moves. For example, three consecutive layouts on the balance beam are considered an E series.

During June, July, and part of August, I worked day and night with Bela and Marta, perfecting my routines, adding new skills, and keeping the fundamentals polished for the judges.

It was during those months of intense training that I found myself tested again and again—not only for my physical skills, but also for my mental toughness. To be a competitive and successful gymnast, you must be totally focused one hundred percent of the time. There are a million details to remember. If you miss one tiny element, you lose your program. It sounds simple, but it's just about the hardest thing anyone can do.

The way we master all these details is to work on every event, twice a day, every day, without variations. It's the only way to see what works and what doesn't. Each and every single time you perform a move, your body position must be exact and consistent. You must be totally precise and predictable in your movements. Only by hundreds and thousands of repetitions can you become so comfortable with a move that you don't have to think about it as much.

Over and over, day in and day out, my teammates and I practice our moves. We repeat each skill again and again and again until it looks and feels just right. One way to practice them is to do "timers," which means doing an abbreviated trick. For example, running down the vault runway and doing only a roundoff back handspring, breaking it off after hitting the springboard instead of following through with a flying skill over the vault. You don't do any flips—you just try to get a feel for the springboard. You do it again and again until that springboard is your best friend. You have to know exactly how much spring it has, how hard you have to bounce on it, how it feels under your bare feet, how slippery it is. . . . Finally it becomes second nature. One benefit of all this knowledge is increased safety. It may look as if we're doing tricky moves, but we only do moves we feel totally comfortable with, that we've practiced a thousand times.

At the 1994 Nationals, as a junior competitor, I was still doing a Yurchenko vault with a half twist. When that competition was over, I felt ready to do more. So during 1995 I worked on doing the Yurchenko with a twist and a half. The twist and a half is an important dismount, and I needed it. A full twist is 360 degrees, and adding a half turn to any twisting dismount is considered difficult and is therefore worth more in the eyes of the judges.

When you try a new skill for the first time, your body has no memory of what it should feel like. So it feels totally weird. You're pushing your body to do something new, and sometimes your body freaks out. For example, I understood *how* to do a twist and a half, so I "told" my body what to do during the vault. But it felt very strange doing it. I felt disoriented, as if my body were lost in space. And my landing was a mess. But then I knew what to work on, what I needed to do to get where I wanted. And I took it from there.

By August I felt very comfortable with the twist and a half. Then I started looking forward to doing a Yurchenko with a double twist! But I knew it wasn't a good idea to push myself, so close to the Nationals. So I stuck with what felt more solid—the full twist and a half.

The weirdness of trying new tricks is another reason our coaches stress that we must do our timers. They help to eliminate the chance of our making a big mistake and getting injured.

Another safety measure is that we always start off doing new tricks on the extra-thick mats, or the soft mats, as we call them at the gym. Only after you feel confident with a skill do you move to the regular mats, like the kind you'd find at a competition. They'll still cushion a fall, but they're not so spongy.

After I felt confident about my vault, I made

rapid progress with the rest of my routines. They were all I thought about. Each day I jumped out of bed already performing my routines in my mind. Then I would race to the gym and go through each element again and again. It started to feel as if I was thinking about my routines *too* much.

At night I actually dreamed about my performance. Sometimes I saw myself doing it in front of the crowd, saw myself doing it well. Sometimes I would dream that I made a mistake and lost points. I began to feel tired all the time, as if I wasn't getting enough rest. I couldn't figure out what was going on.

As it turns out, while I was dreaming, my body was actually trying to perform some of the moves. In my sleep! When I woke up in the morning, I felt as if I had just run a marathon. It became impossible to do my best work in the gym, because I was exhausted and drained from exerting so much energy while I was supposed to be resting. Something had to be done.

7

STRESS BUSTERS

When I finally realized what I was doing to myself by thinking about my routine all the time, I decided I needed to change. It had all happened because I was so anxious, so determined to do my absolute best and to improve my skills more and more. That's not a bad goal—every gymnast, every athlete needs to feel driven. The problem was that I was letting my stress control my body. *I* needed to control my body.

Fortunately, just understanding the problem went a long way to helping me take control. I began to use techniques that enabled me to maintain my top performance in the gym and yet allowed me to relax a bit when I wasn't actually working out.

A big part of the solution was just to get out of

the gym on the weekends. I changed my schedule and got out into the sunshine and fresh air. I tried not to think about my routines. During the week I stuck to my rigorous training, which I really enjoyed. Soon I found that I was back in control and performing better. And I was sleeping better too.

Many of my friends have had the same problem from time to time. So much of our daily life is a strict schedule: Get up, eat, go to the gym, go to school, go back to the gym. Come home, do some schoolwork, and go to bed. For weeks or months you may have the same cycle, over and over. I'm not complaining—most days, I find it fun. I like knowing what to expect and what I need to do. I don't mind the structure. But everyone needs a break sometimes. You have to stop, think about the situation, get focused, and throw yourself back into it. Then you perform better.

I've found that in gymnastics, if you can't deal with the mental stuff, the stress, the emotions, the constant challenges, you can forget about success. This especially applies to competitions. You can have all the perfect workouts that you want in the gym, but if you can't deliver in front of an audience, you won't win. If you can't control your emotions, you might totally blank out when it's your turn to perform. Your mind just goes empty, as if none of your hard work and preparation happened at all.

For a while I had a real problem with that. I was so nervous at competitions that I could never do well. Now I make a real effort to let go of the fear and just try to do my best and enjoy myself. It's taken me a long time to mature, to be able to keep the same focus and confidence at a meet that I feel every day in the gym. But I'm making progress.

8

MY TRAINING
SCHEDULE

The Nationals were only weeks away. I felt confident and prepared. Still, I went to the gym every day and gave it my all. I knew I was improving all the time, day by day, but doing well at the U.S. Championship was the recognition I needed. It would be a real career spark. It would be *my* moment. This gave me the incentive to train as hard as possible during the summer before the meet.

What was especially hard for me at the time was that I was pretty much training solo. I think it's easier and more fun to work with my teammates and friends. We give each other encouragement, and we also provide standards for each other that we can then try to top. But one of my friends, Svetlana Boguinskaia, had returned to Belarus, where she was from. Another good friend, three-time American champion Kim Zmeskal, trained with me for a while, then was unfortunately sidelined with a knee injury. So I was on my own, and I found that hard at times. But after a while I found myself getting used to it—I tried to take the situation and turn it around so that it would be a positive thing for me.

While I was training for the Nationals, I kept the schedule that I still have every day. Each day is tightly planned and pretty hectic. I wake up at six in the morning—sometimes it isn't even light out. I have breakfast at home. Usually it's a homemade bran muffin, juice, and fruit. Athletes must eat healthily, and they must maintain a consistent weight. Because I'm pretty short, only four foot five, a weight of about seventy pounds is healthy for me.

By seven-fifteen, Mom and I hop in the car for the short ride to the gym. Thanks to my parents, I waste very little time going to and from the gym. Our house, in the northern Houston suburbs, is only three or four minutes away from Karolyi's. So we don't even have to allow extra time for rush-hour traffic! If Mom couldn't take me for some reason, I could walk there in ten minutes. It's very convenient. Since I spend six or seven hours a day at Bela's, it's nice to be so close.

(I'll celebrate my fifteenth birthday on September 30, 1996. The year after that, I'll be able to get my learner's permit to drive a car. I can't wait. I know I'm going to love driving. Then I can drive myself to the gym!)

From seven-thirty to ten-thirty, we have morning training at the gym. After we tape up our hands for protection, Kerri, Svetlana Boguinskaia, whoever else is around, and I spend forty-five to fifty minutes conditioning our muscles. We do stretching exercises for flexibility, and we do aerobic exercises to keep us in good shape and get our muscles warmed up. By about eight-twenty, we're ready to start working on our individual routines. We always work on compulsory, or mandatory, elements first—those elements which every gymnast must do in every competition. The moves are decided by the International Gymnastics Federation.

First we practice our compulsory tumbling elements for the floor exercise, then compulsory vaults and uneven parallel bars. At nine-thirty, Marta Karolyi comes and gets us to work on the compulsory beam elements. We do that for about forty-five minutes or more. When you are on the beam, the only voice you hear is Marta's. The beam is her passion, and so is the floor exercise. We hear more from Bela on the uneven bars and the vault, but Marta is always watching and analyzing, no matter what apparatus you are working on.

Finally we work on our compulsory dance movements for the floor exercise. By then it's ten-thirty and time to go home, rest, and have lunch. The mornings just seem to fly by—those three hours feel like five minutes to me.

At home I lie down for a while, and usually try to get some sleep. My body is still young and growing, and I need all the rest I can get. Around eleven-thirty, Mom fixes me lunch—often grilled chicken and a Caesar salad, and fruit. Then I take some time to do my schoolwork, which nowadays I do by video correspondence. (I'll tell you more about that later.)

At two-fifteen, Mom drives me to physical therapy. I do this every day. When an athlete puts her body under as much constant stress as I do, it's a necessity! I *love* physical therapy, even if it's difficult or painful sometimes. Physical therapy involves massages of any sore or strained muscles, heat or ice therapy, and specific exercises to develop and strengthen a particular muscle or muscle group. Sometimes during the massages I practically fall asleep, it feels so good. Other times, if they're massaging a particularly tender or strained muscle, I lie there and grit my teeth. But it hurts in a good way, and I always feel much better afterward. I leave there feeling smooth and relaxed, like a racehorse.

By four o'clock I'm back at the gym for the afternoon training session. The afternoon session is just like the morning session, except that we work on our optional elements instead of our compulsories. Again we warm up and stretch out, and then we practice on each of the apparatuses in turn. Then we work on dance movements and choreography. We often practice in front of large mirrors to get an idea of how we look to an audience. I always practice smiling a lot and looking happy. After all, I feel happy—why shouldn't I show it?

Bela says that my personality—the cheerfulness and joy of performing that come so naturally to me—is one of my greatest strengths as a gymnast. I agree.

Back at home, I have dinner with my family. This is one of my favorite times of the day. I usually eat pretty lightly—just yogurt, or cereal and fruit.

Sometimes my mother will make traditional Romanian food, which I love, and I'll have a small portion of that. Every once in a great while, if I want an extra treat, I'll have a cookie or two, or a piece of chocolate. Yum! During dinner we all get caught up with what each of us is doing, and Christina and I tell my parents what we did in training that day. At Christina's age, six, she is still mostly playing during her lessons at Karolyi's.

She looks up to me and tries to copy everything that I do, which is partly really adorable and partly kind of annoying. Sometimes I get to a point when I just want to say "Okay, please leave me alone for a while now." But Christina still follows me around. Her school friends encourage her. I guess they tell her how lucky she is to have a sister who is doing well in gymnastics. She often tells me how glad she is that we're sisters. It's so sweet! She's also very smart. She seems to know exactly how to persuade people into giving her her way, which is not always easy for a six-year-old.

Mom says that if Christina shows the same promise I did, she and my dad will support Christina's gymnastic ambitions, the way they have mine. I really admire them for that—for all they've done for me, because it disrupts a normal schedule, because so much effort and sacrifice is needed, because so many things have to be put aside so that we can all concentrate on my gymnastics career. But I think they have no regrets. Mom tells me she would do it all over again, with no hesitation. I think it's very important for my parents to feel that they encouraged their children as best they could, that they allowed us to go to the very limit, with their support.

After dinner I might relax for a while, watching my favorite television programs on tape. Knowing how to program a VCR comes with the territory of being a gymnast: Our schedules hardly ever let us watch shows when they come on. Everyone I know is an expert at taping television programs. Two of my favorite shows are *Fresh Prince of Bel-Air* and *Friends.*

Then I might do some more homework, and then I collapse into bed. The next day it starts all over again!

One of Bela's main beliefs is that perfection is within everyone's reach—if you work for it day after day. We, his gymnasts, never doubt that every skill, every routine has to be perfect while we are training. No one in his gym settles for almost-my-best.

By the time one of his gymnasts gets to a competition, the skills come naturally, fluidly, perfectly. For example, Nadia Comaneci, under Bela's coaching back in 1976, achieved the first perfect score of 10.0 ever in Olympic history. And Mary Lou Retton in 1984 scored a 10.0 in the vault, clinching the Olympic title. Any score lower than 10.0 would not have been enough.

It's that little bit extra that wins gold medals. It's digging a little deeper and delivering in those pressure moments, when it really counts, that makes you stand out. That's when the grueling hours of practice pay off.

The pressure moments will always be there. They are expected. But hearing Bela's voice echoing "Perfect! Perfect! Perfect!" helps to keep me sharp. I never want to look back on a moment and say "I wish I could have done it." Nothing is worse than missing the moment.

Most people only know Bela from what they see on television—the excitement he shows when one of his gymnasts throws a good routine, and the big hugs he gives us. What people don't know is that when the television cameras are gone, Bela is still pumped up. Each day he walks into the gym with a big smile on his face, ready to help us do our best. He can always make me laugh when I feel a little down. He seems to know when to tell a joke or say something to make me forget why I'm so frustrated. This upbeat, outgoing nature is a big part of his success.

Everyone has good days and bad days, but Bela is always there to support us and help us in every way he can. Even when I am having a bad day at the gym, a day when my concentration is down and my mistakes are up, Bela and my other coaches keep pushing me, because they want what is best for me. And when they tell me that I can't reach my goals without pushing harder, I know they know what they are talking about, and I believe them. And somehow I reach deeper and push harder. And I'm rewarded.

Without Bela and Marta and the support of my parents, there's no way that, at thirteen, I could have become the youngest United States national gymnastics champion in history.

9

COMPETITIVE SAVVY

At last, in August 1995, the moment had come to go to New Orleans for the U.S. Nationals. After a summer of intensive practice, Bela and Marta told me I was ready. That gave me a lot of confidence, and I believed they were right. I was sure I was ready. After training so much and not competing for a while, it was so exciting to know I was prepared, and to feel all the energy I had inside me as I was waiting to compete. I just had a feeling I would do my best at this meet.

Someone walking into an arena to witness a gymnastics meet for the very first time might have a pretty confused first impression. Unless you know what you're looking for, it probably appears to be a blur of leotards flying through the air, surrounded by chalk dust. Soon enough, though, you realize that gymnastics is the opposite of chaos. It is very structured, very organized, and very careful to hold on to tradition.

That day in August, when my teammates and I walked into the arena, in some ways it felt as if it were my very first meet. I felt an unreal excitement, and also a deep sense of calm. I had released my fears. I felt ready. I would do my best. In the Superdome in New Orleans, as soon as I walked into the main area where we would be competing, everything just clicked. Everything felt right. The atmosphere felt right. The equipment felt right. I even liked my leotard!

As usual, there were all the traditional aspects of a meet. Each meet, no matter if it's small or big, important or less important, follows the same format. First you have a nice long warm-up session. Once your muscles are loose and you feel totally ready, you have to wait for what seems forever in the cold back halls of the arena. This makes me crazy! I feel as if I go from feeling great to feeling tight. I blow on my hands and keep moving, trying to keep as warm as I can. If the wait is too long, I get stiff and my body doesn't want to move fluidly. Many times I've seen a gymnast perform brilliantly during the warm-up, then look terrible in performance. I bet they lost their warmed-up glow. So I keep myself moving, concentrating and as calm as possible.

After the announcements, we athletes march in. We always march in small, synchronized steps, single file, in an orderly, dignified manner. This is one of the first customs every young gymnast must learn. Between events, to get from one apparatus to another, we march in single file. The good thing about marching is that everyone gets to follow a group leader. We never worry about getting confused or lost!

Another precompetition custom I particularly like is singing the National Anthem. I am proud of the United States, proud that I am American. And though there may be a million thoughts running through my mind—something Bela told me, some move I'm thinking of—I always pick up where I left off and sing. It makes me feel good and helps me relax.

When the anthem is over, it's time to compete. Finally! The U.S. Nationals, like all gymnastic competitions, take place in Olympic order. This means vault, uneven bars, balance beam, and floor exercise. We always follow that progression. Some gymnasts, depending on the placement of their performance, will start with the uneven bars or the beam. Then they go through the circle in order until they are back with the event they started on.

For me, the uneven bars are by far the best place to start. Many of my friends feel the same way. It feels better to get the bars and the beam out of the way first, because there is much more pressure associated with them. After they're done, you can concentrate on the floor exercise and vault. I always like to end the day with the vault because I believe I can do my best with this event when I'm totally relaxed. Most of the strain of the competition has been relieved by then.

I always hope for the best, but I never invest a lot of worry in the order that will be drawn for my group. You take what you get. It's all done by random draw, like picking cards out of a hat. At international competitions, the coaches and other people who work with our American federation—USA Gymnastics—meet after the draw to decide the order for our team in each event.

Bela will fight to get his gymnasts the best spots, the spots where he feels we'll do our best for the team and as individuals. He's got that strong personality, and he stands up for what he believes in. I'm glad I'm not another coach, trying to oppose him! All I have to do is concentrate on my own performance.

10

THE VAULT

We began in New Orleans with the all-around competition. This is where each gymnast performs as an individual, not as part of a team. I watched the other gymnasts perform, silently congratulating them or critiquing their performances. I tried to stay focused and loose. I tried to stay upbeat and positive. Somewhere in the stands, my parents and my little sister were watching me. But I couldn't think about that right now. I had to stay in the present.

It seemed both as if my turn came in mere seconds and as if it arrived only after agonizing hours of waiting. Time was compressed and elongated because of the excitement of the meet.

I would begin with the vault. As I awaited my

turn at the end of the vault runway, I tried to keep my legs warm so that I wouldn't totally freeze up. I kept thinking of everything I had to do—all the small, precise puzzle pieces, each one of which must be perfect for me to compete successfully. And of course, Bela was there with me, reminding me what to do, pumping up my adrenaline.

"Okay! Okay! You can do it, Domi. You can do it!"

I felt that I had done the vault routine so many times that I would be successful. But Bela always gets so excited at competitions. And he's been to so many meets that he knows what it takes—he wants to make sure I'm psyched up when it really counts.

It was my turn. I faced the judges and saluted in the American way, with both arms raised high and straight above my head. (Europeans salute with one arm.) Of course, I had practiced even this salute a hundred times, back at Bela's ranch. Bela and Marta sit behind a table and pretend to be judges, and we gymnasts take turns saluting. You want your salute to say "I'm ready! Watch what I can do!" instead of "Boy, am I scared." It's important to have a confident appearance.

After my salute, I waited for the green light.

That's the signal that my time has really come. Gymnasts in a meet have to be cautious and wait for this signal. If you begin before the green light flashes, the judges can, and will, penalize you with a score of zero. For the vault competition, female gymnasts get two tries. You must always do your best on each attempt. If you get a zero on one vault, it can destroy your concentration and end your chance to win a title or a medal. So we are often reminded that, no matter how nervous we are, we must never fail to wait for the signal.

The vault runway is eighty feet long, but not every gymnast starts from the very end. Where you start depends on your body type, how fast you run, and mostly, what is comfortable. There is a measuring tape placed down one side, and that's where you find your mark. I always take my mark seventy-eight feet from the springboard, left foot first. When I compete outside the United States, I take my mark twenty-four meters from the springboard.

I began to run down the runway. I always run as fast as I can because it helps me achieve the greatest possible speed going off the springboard for my back handspring over the vault. I love the sensation of flying as I try to get as much height as possible. Height

My mother, Camelia, cradled me in her arms when I was a
newborn, while my proud father, Dimitry, looked on.

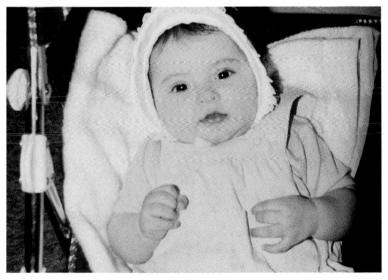

When I was three months old, my parents took me for a spin
in my stroller in Hollywood, California.

I was only six months old when my parents tested my strength by having me hold on to a clothesline. I never let go. Of course, my parents were ready to catch me if I did.

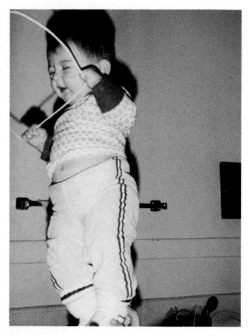

I took my first steps at age one, and was quite a walker by sixteen months. Maybe I was already practicing my floor exercise routine!

Birthdays are great. Here I am celebrating my first birthday with my mother and family friends.

My little sister, Christina, is adorable—even if she doesn't look too happy that I'm making her pose for the camera.

A family portrait, 1995 (left to right): Dimitry, Dominique, Christina, and Camelia.

Christina and I had a blast clowning around at the 1995 Ringling Bros. and Barnum & Bailey Circus in Houston.

Hanging out at the beach ranks high on my list of favorite things to do. I go to Padre Island in Texas with my family whenever I can.

At age eleven, I was the youngest gymnast ever to compete at the 1992 Pan-American games in São Paulo, Brazil, where I captured five medals. Gold medals: all-around, floor exercise, uneven bars, vault; silver medal: balance beam.

I loved competing in front of the crowd at the 1992 Pan-American games in São Paulo, Brazil, where I won a gold medal for my floor exercise.

The balance beam is one of my favorite events.

My coach, Bela Karolyi, got me pumped up during the 1995 U.S. World Team Trials.

Fellow American gymnasts Jaycie Phelps and Shannon Miller were happy for me when I won the all-around title at the 1995 U.S. World Team Trials.

I always feel a real adrenaline rush during my floor routine.
(1995 World Championship)

Along with the entire U.S. gymnastic team, I received a *gi* (the yellow garment) from the mayor of Fukui City, Japan, when we competed in the 1995 World Championships in nearby Sabae. We all wore the *gi*s when we attended a reception in our honor.

© DAVE BLACK 1996

With Bela spotting me, I'm never afraid to fly through my uneven bars routine. (1995 World Championship)

It's always exciting—and a little scary—to do risky moves on the balance beam. (1995 World Championship)

Along with the balance beam, the floor exercise is my favorite event. I love getting the crowd into my routine. (1995 World Championship)

© DAVE BLACK 1996

I was thrilled when my balance beam routine at the 1995 World Championship earned me a tie for the silver medal.

© DAVE BLACK 1996

I was extremely proud to stand on the winners' platform during the medal ceremony for the balance beam (1995 World
Championship). Lilia Podkopayeva of Ukraine and I tied for
the silver medal; Mo Huilan of China (back) won the gold.

and distance are two things you need for a successful vault, but general technique and sticking the landing—landing solidly without taking a step—count for a great deal also. General technique is extremely important. What you do in the blink of an eye, from the springboard to pushing off the vault, to landing on the mat, will make the difference between a mediocre score and a great one.

I've found the surest way to perform a vault exactly as I did back at the gym is to "feel" my steps on the runway. I rely on muscle memory to take me through. That's why the warm-up period is so important. If you can get the right feel running down the runway, muscle memory will take over when you hit the springboard. No matter where you are, you will suddenly feel at home, because you've done exactly the same thing thousands of times before.

I performed my Yurchenko with a twist and a half. I ran as fast as I could, did a back handspring off the springboard, flew through the air, and pushed off the vault as hard as I could. I could immediately sense that I had achieved great height and was perfectly positioned to go into the twisting movement. My body took over, coming out of the twist at precisely the right second. Then I automatically put my feet down and bent my knees to absorb the shock of landing. Instantly I straightened up, arched my back, and threw my hands over my head. I had done well! I had done my best, I could feel it. Even before I turned to look at the judges, I searched for Bela's face. His big smile told me what I already knew.

For that vault, I received a score of 9.9, very close to perfection. I was happy.

11

THE UNEVEN PARALLEL BARS

From the vault to the uneven bars, it was rush, rush, rush. There is more equipment involved in performing a bars routine than there is in any of the other events. The apparatus is more difficult to move; there are mats, and the bars are often adjusted slightly for the individual gymnast.

For the gymnast there is also more preparation. Before my turn on the bars I placed grips over the palms of my hands. This helps prevent my calluses from ripping open when I'm holding tightly to the bars. I also add wrist supports. To perform safely at a high level of difficulty, both these things must be in place. Some gymnasts tape their fingers together for extra support. I use a piece of rubbery, padded material called neoprene over each wrist. The friction of your skin sliding against the bars during a routine can give you brush burns, or even little rips, so extra cushioning is important. Sometimes I add another layer of prewrap, which is very thin plastic that you can fold up and put over parts of your wrist that are especially sensitive.

One of Bela's coaches gives me two neoprene wrist protectors every Christmas. They usually last me the year. I also keep a small supply of rubber bands to hold my fingers together in case my grips get loose while I'm on the bars. You have to be prepared for everything. If your grips aren't applied perfectly, a bars routine can go from perfection to disaster in a big hurry.

While I was quickly putting on my protective equipment, Bela was rubbing my shoulders, keeping me loose, giving me encouragement. I added a little chalk and water to my fingers to make sure I'd have enough traction on the smooth wood. Then it was my turn.

I saluted the judges.

Bela gave me a little push toward the bars. "Go!" he said. "You can do it. You know you are ready."

The uneven bars is the event I worry about more than any other, so I said a little extra prayer right before I began my routine. I've always had to work the hardest on the bars to make the routines perfect. I can do the skills well enough, so I'm not sure why I have a little alarm that goes off about the bars. In fact, when I was younger, back in Florida, I had lots of fun on the bars, just playing, doing one skill after another. Of course, I was doing everything wrong, with bad technique.

When I first came to Houston, Bela and Marta saw my bars routine and just looked at each other. I could tell they were thinking, "We're going to have a hard time with this one." I had no technique, no maturity. But I was only ten years old—I had a lot to learn.

For the U.S. Nationals, I mounted, then did a kip-cast handstand on the lower bar. You have to get that bar the first time or the judges will deduct from your score. I managed to get a firm grip on the bar. Then I did a Poshikova, which was my first big skill on that event. I flew up to the high bar and caught it squarely. Then I swung back and did a back salto. Sometimes in practice I'm a little forward or a little behind on the rotation, but this time I felt I had gotten it just right. All those days of repetitive training were showing.

Next I leaned back and did a pirouette with a

handstand into an uprise, another handstand, then a giant flip. I followed that with a Geinger, which is a flying release move where you let go of the bar and catch it as you rotate around. I really have to work on that one—it's not one of my best skills. For some reason, ever since I was little, I've had poor technique on the Geinger.

(In case you were wondering, the Poshikova, salto, and Geinger are all moves named after famous former gymnasts.)

After the Geinger, I went back into a big swing, performed a jam to get from the low bar to the high bar, then did a handstand and two giant swings. My dismount was a double layout onto the mat. I had wanted to add a full twist to the dismount, but usually I feel so dead by the end of the bars routine that I can't find the energy to add anything extra. My arms felt as if they couldn't hold on to anything. I plan to work on that in the future.

As in the vault, I stuck my dismount. I threw my arms over my head. I could tell in my bones that I had done well—I had even done a very good Geinger.

Now I had one more very difficult routine to perform—the balance beam—before I could look forward to the joy of the floor exercise.

12

THE BALANCE BEAM

The first thing I had to do after my bars routine was rip off all my padding and wrist guards and palm protectors. All that stuff is useless, even a hindrance, on the beam. The only thing I needed was a pair of beam shoes, and I quickly slipped them on and ran to get into place.

Many gymnasts perform on the beam barefoot. When I was younger, I did too. Then I developed a problem with the middle toe on my left foot. The skin underneath it cracked and split from the pressure of my routine. Since I worked out every day, it could never heal. You might think that a small sore spot on one toe isn't a big deal, but it's a great big deal when you're a gymnast. Each time I got on the beam, my toe began killing me. Finally it became so painful that I couldn't ignore it. (And I can ignore a lot of pain, through concentration and practice.)

As soon as I started wearing beam shoes, it made all the difference. My toe healed. Now I never have a problem. Beam shoes are a little like ballet slippers but with a more rigid bottom. When I wear them, I can't point my feet quite as well. I have to concentrate more to make sure the line of my foot looks fully extended, the way it should be. But they do what they're supposed to do: protect my feet.

Before the beam event, each gymnast gets a thirty-second touch, which is a very brief warm-up on the beam during which you can practice just a few skills. I did that, jumped down, and got ready to perform my routine.

To start my program, I took a short run off the springboard and did a pirouette onto the beam, landing with all my weight on my shoulders. This move is called the Silivas, after a Romanian gymnast named Daniela Silivas. She was a gold medalist on the beam at the 1988 Olympics. I think it's a great move, and it's a very dramatic beginning.

After the Silivas, I did a little roll, and then I was up on my feet, on a wooden beam only four inches wide, four feet from the ground. Every moment up there requires nothing less than total concentration.

I did a series of dance movements down to one end of the beam. These dance movements let the judges see my flexibility, balance, grace, and control. At the end of the beam, I turned so that my heels were about an inch and a half from the back edge. Usually there is a thin layer of chalk dust on the beam, so I make a tiny scratch mark with my fingernail during a practice. I use this mark to keep my bearings, and to stay away from the very edge.

From there I went into my flight series, always beginning with my left foot. (I am a left-footed gymnast who is right-handed most of the time. Strange but true!) The flight series began with a back handspring, hands on the beam as I made the rotation. Then I performed three consecutive layouts—no hands, just aerial backward flips—with a slight arch in my body position. This is usually the part that makes coaches and parents hold their breaths, but it wasn't the end of my routine.

I performed another series of dance movements, including my compulsory leap jumps for an added degree of difficulty. After the dance movements, I added something new: a back handspring into consecutive handstand pirouettes. It was a new skill, and no one else had done it in competition before. (If I decide to use it in the Olympics, it will be named after me. Someday, perhaps, little girls will be performing the Moceanu on the beam. That's so exciting to think about.)

During my whole beam routine, I was thinking of Marta. If I wanted to make her happy, I had to do well on the beam. I was so anxious not to disappoint her, not to disappoint myself. It's the event she loves the most, and I wanted to show her that I loved it too. Finally came my dismount. I flung myself into it with all my power, trying to keep a perfectly controlled landing. And I stuck! I could almost hear Marta's cries of happiness and encouragement as I threw my arms overhead.

And that made three routines down, one more to go: the floor exercise.

13

THE FLOOR EXERCISE

After the first three events, I knew I was ahead by a small margin. If I could turn in a good floor exercise, I had a chance at a medal—possibly even a gold one. The floor routine is one of my very favorites—I'm filled with joy when I'm out there performing. More than any other event, it's a chance for me to show my stuff and engage the audience in my performance.

I was so excited about going out there and wowing the crowd that I didn't feel at all nervous or excited. A big change from my earlier meets! I had no worries. I'm not sure how that was true. It's probably hard to imagine facing the performance of your life, the one that will make or break you—and in front of tens of thousands of people, no less—and not feel hysterical, but it was definitely true for me.

I felt supremely confident. I knew I could do every trick, every move in my routine. They came easily to me after so many months of training. So when I headed out on the floor, I decided to show it off really big, really powerfully from the moment I saluted the judges. Even better, I was the last competitor in that event, so I could really go after the crowd. I was determined to get the attention of everyone in the arena.

Bela seemed to sense my mood, and he encouraged it. He believed I could deliver a great performance. "You can do it, Dominique, with no problem," he told me over and over. "You know you are the best. Show the people you are the best."

As soon as the music started I was psyched. Bela had chosen "Chantilly Lace" by the Big Bopper as my signature song, and I loved it. The catchy rhythm and fun words made me feel like snapping my fingers.

The floor exercise takes place on a square of carpet forty feet by forty feet. The object is to perform all your skills, using as much of the carpet as possible, without putting even a pinkie toe over the line.

I began with a dance sequence cued to the music, which led into a tumbling pass from one corner of the carpet to its opposite diagonal corner. In my routine that day, there were a total of four tumbling passes from corner to corner. I used handsprings, roundoffs, layouts, saltos, you name it. I nailed every one. On one of the passes I performed my trademark move, which is a little hop at the very end of the tumbling series. It starts with a handspring, front full twist, followed by a forward punch layout (no arms, body straight). On the landing after the layout, instead of raising my arms to signal the finish, I jumped straight up into the air, landed, then went into my final pose. The crowd went crazy, clapping, whistling, calling my name.

(I picked that move up from Svetlana Boguinskaia, who had been training with me and Kerri Strug at Bela's. I noticed that when Svetlana practiced different passes on her floor routine, she did that little hop move at the end. She did this only in the gym, not in competitions. After a while I added it to my performance, just to give it a different look.

Svetlana is planning to represent the Republic of Belarus in the Summer Games in Atlanta.)

As soon as I landed my final pose cleanly, I felt ecstatic. I felt in my heart that I would win the all-around. I had done my best.

Yes! I thought. The moment I've been waiting for my whole life is here! I could barely breathe as I waited for my floor exercise score.

Then it came: 9.80. I confess that I was a little surprised and disappointed. I felt that I had done better than that. I guess the crowd agreed with me, because they booed the judges' decision.

But even that score was good enough to win the all-around gold medal—over a great gymnast and 1992 Olympic silver medalist, Shannon Miller from Oklahoma. I had a total all-around score of 78.45. Shannon's was 78.25.

There's no way to describe the excitement I felt at that moment, when I realized I had definitely won the gold. Bela rushed over and swept me up into one of his huge bear hugs.

"You did it!" he shouted into my ear. "You did it! You little sucker, you did it!"

I was melting with happiness to hear his words.

And I knew that up in the stands, my parents and my little sister were happy for me and proud of me. I felt that they could really see what all their sacrifices and endless support had led to.

Dominique Moceanu, United States National Gymnastics Senior Champion.

It was a tremendous moment.

14

FAME AND FANS

When you win a competition as big as the U.S. National Championships, it's great, and it makes you feel great. But a title like that comes with a price: From that day on, you have to work even harder.

I would never want people to think that I was complaining about being the national champion. It's a joy for me to be recognized as my country's top female gymnast. It was a great satisfaction to accomplish the goal I had been working toward for so long. I'm very proud of achieving the level of success that I did in New Orleans.

But I also know that I didn't get there alone. Only one person, me, stood on the top step of the awards platform, but many people deserved to stand there too. My parents, for their generous support and sacrifice; my coaches, who have constantly worked with me and pushed me to be my best; and my friends and teammates, who have been so helpful and supportive.

Where would I be today if my parents hadn't decided to move to Houston to give me the chance to work with Bela? Where would I be if I hadn't received the best coaching at the best facility? Getting me to that top awards step took a lot of effort on everyone's part. It took a team.

After the Nationals, it was a little hard to get back to business as usual. Bela was so pleased and happy for me, but remember, he's coached gymnasts who have won gold medals at the *Olympics*.

At first I felt two things: One, that I was suddenly under new pressure, the pressure to stay number one. And two, that it was strange to find myself back at the gym, getting up early and doing my compulsories with the others.

Now I realize that it is almost guaranteed that you will struggle with training after you come down from the tremendous high of winning a major meet. At the time I didn't know what was wrong with me.

I struggled for quite a few days in the gym, even though a part of me was glad to return to my daily routine.

Of course, Bela knows how tempting it is to slack off after a big meet. That's where his experience in working with so many great gymnasts is especially valuable. He knew what I was feeling, and he let me know that he wouldn't tolerate anything less than my best. National champion or novice, you must continue to train on a regular schedule. Gymnastics is a fragile sport. Disciplined repetition is the only way to stay sharp and keep moving forward.

As time went on, I got back into my old rhythms. I found joy in my regular workouts with my friends and teammates. I set new goals for myself and worked to achieve them. I remembered Karolyi's Law: You can always do better.

One thing that was exciting to me was that Betty Okino, Kerri Strug, Kim Zmeskal, and I all moved to the blue gym. It was finally finished, and boy, is it fabulous.

In the tan gyms, I worked among dozens of other girls of all ages and at all levels of training. At the blue gym you know you're aiming for the top competitions, such as the Nationals, the Worlds, and the

Olympics. Each of us elite gymnasts has plenty of privacy in the blue gym, and we each have our own individual set of equipment. For example, I have my very own balance beam and my own uneven bars—just for me. It's incredible! Everything is the very best there is. Just walking into the blue gym makes me feel special, which is why Bela built it. He wants his elite gymnasts, his champions, to have every chance available to improve. The blue gym allows us to train with no distractions. I love the setup, and I think it definitely provides inspiration to younger gymnasts. Everyone wants to be chosen for the blue gym.

I found that the excitement and fame of my success in New Orleans continued even after I got back to training. My hard work and discipline had won me the title and helped me mature. Which was a good thing, because I now had the new pressures of increased publicity.

Suddenly tons of people wanted to interview me. Being a good interview subject is a skill like any other, and it took me a while to learn it. Reporters expected me to be able to handle myself with them as well as I could against a competitor. At first that was difficult for me. Now I find the words coming more naturally, because I've been answering questions constantly. My new ease with reporters is one of the many good things that came out of winning the Nationals.

Another really wonderful thing that happened was that I began to get real fans—fans who wrote me letters. I realized that people from all over the country felt a special bond with me. It was totally unexpected and amazing. I get fan letters from people who say that they love me and watch me on television and collect pictures of me. It's incredible to have such an impact on others. I just try not to get too freaked out by it. But I love knowing that I'm helping kids by showing them it's really possible to succeed and still have fun.

The kids who write to me are definitely psyched about gymnastics, and they feel a huge surge of excitement when they see me. And I try to give back just as much as I get. I really love this sport, and when I go out there to compete, the smile on my face is no acting job. I sincerely love being out there, and I believe every kid should make that the number one reason for competing, whether as a gymnast or in any other sport.

That's why I try so hard to answer my fan mail, although sometimes it piles up so fast that I get behind. The mail comes to Bela's gym. Sometimes my mom and I laugh and wonder how some of the mail even finds me. Kids often just write my name and "Houston, Texas," on the envelope, or just "Karolyi's Gym" with no street address. It's like mail addressed to Santa Claus: Somehow it gets where it needs to go.

My mother enjoys my fan mail as much as I do. I always kid her about how she loves to read the letters and how happy it makes her to see how much kids care for me. People say such nice things in their letters, such sweet and thoughtful comments. I read as many as I can in between my other responsibilities.

My fans seem to be of all ages. Sometimes parents type a letter at their child's request. Some kids write their letters using really big printing, and I'm always touched by how much effort it took. I even get mail from teenagers. I have one fan, a girl older than I am, who writes me long letters on beautiful, flower-bordered stationery. Letters also come sometimes from adults. Reading them means everything to me. Their words of encouragement always make me want to go to the gym and work harder.

Sometimes kids write to ask me for advice about

how they can get ahead in gymnastics. I always tell them to just try to have fun. Don't be pressured, don't make yourself miserable with pushing yourself ahead. Do what you enjoy for as long as you enjoy it. If you're not having a great time, then something's wrong, and you should find something you enjoy more. This is a sport for people who love it.

My being seen on television has made a big difference in the amount of my fan mail. And out in public, in a shopping mall or an airport, I've noticed a change this year in the number of people who recognize me or look at me curiously. Not everyone is sure exactly what my name is or how it's pronounced, but they'll stop for a moment and say nice things, such as "We're so proud of you!" and "Hope you do well this year!"

The extra attention I get is cool, and I have to tell the truth: I like it. It's so nice that someone wants an autograph, wants to say an encouraging word or two. I guess it's all part of being an athlete, a public figure.

But even though I may like it, I refuse to get bigheaded about it. No matter when or where someone comes up to me, the most important thing is to be thankful for their kindness. I know I may not be in the public eye forever. My parents feel that one of the most important lessons I need to remember is to stay modest, no matter how good I am. They stress that I need to stay levelheaded, that I have to be a real person. Gymnastics is only one part of my life, and I have to be able to live all the rest of my life with my other qualities.

I wanted to share with you a small selection from some of the letters that have meant the most to me:

I'm proud of you, whether you score a 10.0 or a 9.0. I don't care . . . because I can tell that you put so much effort into your work. Your self-discipline amazes me and, in my heart, I truly believe that you're [a] champion.

I hope you read all of my letters and cards because [they are] all very personal and are meant especially for you. I hope you write back soon.

(From Honolulu, Hawaii, December 1995)

Dominique, you have captured the . . . spirit of the United States. God has blessed you with an enormous amount of talent, energy, and goodwill. You have a happy, positive attitude, which is contagious! After the tragic news of two weeks ago from

Oklahoma City [the April 19 bombing], and seeing the senseless destruction of human life, especially the children, you lifted my spirits and my heart.

Remember, the level of excellence you have achieved and the heights you will reach goes beyond the sport of gymnastics. You are destined to become one of the greatest athletes in the world. You will someday be an inspiration to millions. You are a great gymnast and a beautiful person.

(From Mays Landing, New Jersey, May 1995)

I am always so thankful for such kind and encouraging words, and hope that I will continue to be the type of champion and the kind of person who makes Americans feel proud.

15

MY NORMAL LIFE

After the Nationals, after I settled down into my regular routine at the gym, I settled down into a more normal home life too. For example, I tried to get caught up in my schoolwork.

I started ninth grade in the fall of 1995, but this school year has been different from any that I've had before. For one thing, I had a late start after qualifying for my first World Championship. The 1995 Worlds were hosted by Sabae, Japan, during the first ten days of October. So right after I got back into the swing of things, I had to go into precompetition frenzy again!

I spent the month of September getting ready for that meet, while other kids were starting back to school. By then my parents and I had already made the decision that I would spend the months leading up to the Summer Olympics taking ninth-grade courses by the correspondence method. This method of learning is better than ever because the materials have been adapted to videotape. This allows me to "go to class" with an actual teacher who appears on the television screen. The best part of video correspondence is being able to rewind the tape when something is hard to understand or when I want to hear or see something again.

Each videotape contains a series of subjects and individual classes for every day of the week. This beats just reading materials and doing homework assignments. I feel as if I can learn as well as or even better than if I were in a regular classroom with other kids. And the tapes present the homework assignments so that my mother or father can work with me if I need extra help.

But it's still not as easy as it sounds. When I went to a real school, I had more friends, and took part in some nongymnastic activities. With video correspondence, I need a lot more discipline. Some days, especially if I've had a difficult time in the gym, the last thing I feel like doing when I get home is going up to my room, putting in a tape, and learning about math! So sometimes I have to really push myself, the way I do with gymnastics, to watch what I need to watch and learn what I need to learn.

Math is a hard subject for me. I really get frustrated when I can't do a math assignment. On the other hand, I'm a great speller, which helps me with reading and writing.

I feel that the discipline of training to compete in gymnastics makes me a better student, and I think that's true for other athletes too. When I attended public school, the kids who participated seriously in sports always seemed more involved in the classroom, while some of the other kids seemed to be goofing off. From being in gymnastics classes, I knew how to behave, how to concentrate and pay attention. Can you imagine Bela's face if I was joking around or talking to other kids or not paying attention? I don't even want to think about it! But some kids do exactly that in school classes. I don't know how they expect to do well or get ahead.

As thrilled as I am to train at the best gym in the world, and to have the chance to rise up the senior division to the National Championship, still, I do look forward to going back to regular school, probably next year. I miss seeing my nongymnast friends every day. My short-term plans are to qualify for the Olympic team, for the 1996 Summer Olympics. After the Olympics, there are plans for a national tour of Olympic gymnasts that is scheduled to last two or three months. Plus there may be additional competitions. So I'm not likely to be back in regular school as a classroom student until the beginning of 1997. If all goes well, that's the plan.

Although gymnastics means a great deal to me, I don't ignore the importance of education. In the future, I'd like to attend college and study sports medicine. I already enjoy studying the human body, anatomy, and science. Gymnasts necessarily are very familiar with their bodies and how they work; we learn about the various muscle groups, bones, and joints at a young age.

Right now my focus is gymnastics, and it's practically my whole world. But a gymnastics career doesn't last forever. As my body ages and changes, gymnastics will become less of an option for me. When that time comes, I have another life, another career planned. Right now, I'm still working on achieving my gymnastics goals. And that is helping to prepare me for what comes later.

16
DOWNTIME

When I'm not at the gym, one of my favorite things to do is just to relax quietly in my room, listening to music. Sometimes it seems as if I hardly ever have time to do this! The demands of training, schoolwork, competitions, public appearances—they all leave me very little free time.

But my parents and I try to make sure I do get the occasional chance to decompress. Being able to totally unwind sometimes is the key to being able to handle increased stress at other times.

I love being in my room at home. That's where I keep all my souvenirs, all my collections. My parents are even expanding my room toward the back of the house so that I'll have plenty of space for everything! I can't bear to throw anything away.

I have a collection of small stuffed animals, especially elephants. I also collect souvenir spoons from different cities I've visited or competed in. And I'm not that superstitious, but I have a collection of guardian angel pins. Wherever I'm traveling or shopping somewhere, I look for them, and sometimes my mother finds them for me too. Seven is my lucky number, so I have seven small guardian angel pins attached to the outside of the little canvas gym bag that goes everywhere with me. USA Gymnastics gave it to me a long time ago, and even though it's worn and faded and has a tricky zipper, I'm sentimental about it and won't trade it in. (Okay, so maybe I *am* a little superstitious!)

Besides shopping for clothes (I love clothes!), I also enjoy getting new music CDs. Since I've lived in Texas, I learned to love country-and-western music. Some of my favorite musicians are Garth Brooks, George Strait, and Reba McIntyre. Most of my fellow gymnasts are into country music also. At the gym we listen to music all day long, so we try to have a lot of variety. We always tease Bela about liking rock-and-roll oldies. He's the one who found "Chantilly Lace" for me.

Sometimes, though, if I have a little downtime, I

don't listen to music or watch my television programs. Every once in a while I just take a break from everything and sit in my room, thinking back over all my happy memories and all the good things that have happened in past years.

Along the top of one wall in my room I hang most of my gymnastics medals. The really special medals, such as the ones from the U.S. National Championships and the World Championships, I keep in velvet-covered cases on a shelf.

On another wall (next to my *Legends of the Fall* Brad Pitt poster), there is a framed article about me that *Sports Illustrated* did after I won my first senior National Championship.

Out in our living room, there is one bookcase where we keep mementos of my gymnastics career. There are framed photographs and trophies that have a special meaning for me. For example, there's a picture of me from the 1995 World Championships in Japan, framed with large letters that spell my name in Japanese. And there's my Athlete of the Year trophy that USA Gymnastics gave me in 1995. *Sports Illustrated* magazine also gave me an engraved sterling silver bowl after I was featured in its "Faces in the Crowd" section as an up-and-coming athlete.

My parents also keep a scrapbook for me, full of photographs, news clippings, magazine articles, competition programs, you name it. It's pretty full by now! I look forward to the day when I can pull it out and show my children what I accomplished.

All these things have happy memories attached to them, and I know I'll enjoy looking at them and remembering those times long after I've moved on to another career.

17

I'M A FAN TOO

Besides doing gymnastics, I enjoy other sports too. If there's no gymnastics on television, then I'm perfectly happy to watch ice-skating or tennis. Sometimes I play tennis, which is a lot of fun. And one of my favorite photographs is of Monica Seles. She signed it for me and wrote on it, "Hope to meet you in Atlanta! Take care." I really do hope we run into each other at the Olympics. I'm a huge fan of hers.

Ice-skating might be my second-favorite sport, after gymnastics. The two sports make many of the same physical demands. I know how to ice-skate, how to glide around and make little circles without falling. But, as with most other sports, I don't try to do too much. I can't risk an injury at this point in my life. Bela would have very little patience with me if I arrived at the gym with an ice-skating injury! I can just see his face now!

Still, it's very safe for me to *watch* ice-skating on television. Some of my favorite skaters are Kristi Yamaguchi, Kurt Browning, and Scott Hamilton. I met them at the Rock 'n' Roll Championship for skaters and gymnasts. (I won a real electric guitar at that show! I keep it in my room.)

It was exciting for me to meet them and discover how nice they are. I'm also a big fan of Michelle Kwan and Tara Lipinski. I saw Tara on television when she was skating in the World Championships, and it was easy to root for her, since she reminded me of myself. For one thing, she's pretty tiny. We're small people with big hearts and bigger dreams.

18

ON THE GO

I think one of the absolute best things about being involved with competitive-level gymnastics is the opportunity to travel to new places and meet new people. There are times when I travel with my team to a new city, but we're so busy all the time we're there, we don't have much of a chance to explore! So I make a mental note to myself to come back someday and really look around. Traveling and seeing new things is a big part of my education. It's impossible to be close-minded when you see many different cultures and heritages.

So far in my competitive life I've traveled to Sabae, Japan, to São Paulo, Brazil, and to Charleroi, Belgium. Those are three very different places!

In Sabae, as usual, I didn't have a lot of time to

sight-see. Mostly what I saw of the city was from bus windows as I was going back and forth between the arena and my hotel. One of the things that impressed me most about Japan, even in the airport, is that it is amazingly clean. There is no trash around. The floors are clean. The streets are clean. There is no graffiti. And the people there seem so well-mannered—they always wait in line politely, with no pushing or shoving. When my teammates and I would walk down the street to the bus, hundreds of people would line up just to ask for autographs. They would touch me gently on the shoulder in a gesture of respect. People there seem much more restrained than Americans. I think America has more freedom of expression, and of individuality, but I do wish Americans littered less and didn't mess up public spaces.

What I saw of Japan from bus windows was very pretty. It is very different-looking from any place I had ever seen before. There were hills and interesting Japanese-style buildings. The modern buildings looked just like modern buildings everywhere, but I saw a few old-fashioned ones that looked as if they were out of pictures, with their funny, upturned roofs.

While I was in Sabae, the governor held a reception for all of us foreign competitors. It was really fun. We all wore yellow traditional Japanese *gis*. I thought we looked like colorful butterflies. We ate traditional Japanese food. I ate mostly rice. I wouldn't try the jellyfish! It was a great opportunity to get a little taste of the culture. It's definitely on my list of places to return to someday.

While I like traveling to different places, sometimes it's hard to deal with jet lag. My body is very used to being on a particular schedule, and when I suddenly put it on a completely different schedule, it weirds out. I usually get used to the new time zone pretty quickly, though.

I'm very lucky that usually at least one of my parents can travel with me. Some girls aren't so lucky, and I know they miss their parents terribly when they're away. But having my parents with me makes me much less homesick. Home is where *they* are!

When I travel with my teammates, even if my parents are with me, I always share a room with another gymnast. This helps me stay focused on the reason we're there. You might think two girls in a hotel room equals a party, but I'm afraid not. We have to be very, very serious. We need to get enough rest and eat sensibly so that we'll be at our absolute best when we perform. When we have a tiny bit of free time I rush to buy postcards—some to save, some to send to all my friends back home. I also buy little spoons for my collection, or other small things that are neat. I always try to buy presents for my parents, my sister, and my best friends.

For the Pan-American games in 1992, I traveled to São Paulo, Brazil. I had a great time at the meet, and afterward we actually got a whole day to sightsee. We immediately went to the beach, which was beautiful and clean, with clear turquoise water. I love being at the beach. The waves are so relaxing, and I enjoy being out in the sun, since I don't get to do it very much.

The Brazilians I met were very warm and demonstrative, and were much more open than the Japanese. They didn't hesitate to come up to us and ask for autographs, and wanted to hug us and touch us. I got the impression that people in Brazil are looser and less concerned with appearances—more interested in living well and being happy. But that was just the quick impression I got.

In Belgium in 1993, we were in a town called Charleroi for two weeks for an invitational meet. Charleroi is just about the most old-fashioned-looking town I've ever seen. It looked ancient. The buildings, although they were kept up well, just looked very old to me. The streets were very narrow and winding, as if they had been made for horses and carriages. But of course there were no horses and carriages. People drove cars—very small cars.

The hotel we stayed in was really funny. For one thing, my room was so tiny that I could cross it in about ten steps. (And I have little feet!) The phone was very big and old-fashioned, and I could never get it to work properly. The television was like a TV from *I Love Lucy*—big and old and black-and-white, with antennas. There were four channels, all of them in either French or Flemish, which are the two languages they speak in Belgium. And since I hadn't brushed up on either my Flemish or my French before I came . . . let's just say I didn't watch a lot of television.

The weirdest thing was that the bathroom was *down the hall* from my room. No one had their own bathroom in their room. So to shower or whatever, you had to leave your room, troop down the hall, unlock the door, and then make your way back again. My own room had a special code that I needed to enter to get back in, and for some reason I had a hard time remembering it. More than once I got up in the middle of the night, practically sleepwalked my way down the hall, got some water, and groped my way back to my room, only to find that I was locked out. It was pretty embarrassing, but fortunately I wasn't the only one who went through the same experience. I'm not naming any names, though!

But even with all the cultural differences and the jet lag and the things to get used to, I still love traveling.

My family and I haven't taken a vacation since I was ten—we've been too busy! But there are a bunch of places I'd really like to see someday. For example, I was at Disney World briefly for an exhibition, but I would love to spend a week there. I bet my sister would love it too. I'm also crazy about the beach. That might be my favorite kind of vacation. I hope to go to the Cayman Islands someday. (They are between Cuba and Jamaica.) The beaches look beautiful. And as I said before, I'd like to revisit all the places I've gone to for competitions, and this time have enough leisure to really explore them.

Right now, though, I'm looking forward to going to Atlanta!

19

COUNTDOWN TO
THE OLYMPICS

No one can become a competitive athlete without being influenced by athletes who came before him or her. But while people often refer to the striking physical resemblance I have to Nadia Comaneci, or say that the joy I show during competition reminds them of Mary Lou Retton, I've never really compared myself to either of them. I'm familiar with their incredible accomplishments, of course, and I admire them greatly, but I take my day-to-day inspiration from gymnasts who are performing now.

The first gymnast whose name I connected with and whom I can clearly remember watching on television was Kim Zmeskal. She won three U.S. Championships (in 1990, '91, and '92) and the all-around title in the Worlds in 1991, and helped the United

States win a team bronze at the 1992 Summer Olympics in Barcelona, Spain. I watched as much of that competition as I could. It was so exciting to see Kim and Kerri Strug and Betty Okino—gymnasts I worked with daily at Karolyi's—wearing their Olympic uniforms and representing our country. These three gymnasts are the ones I admire most, and they influenced me to pursue the same goals when I first joined Karolyi's Gymnastics.

Since then, I've had the chance to meet Mary Lou Retton. Of course, I had seen a tape of her great moment at the 1984 Olympics, and about a million posters of her. There probably isn't a single gymnastics club in America that doesn't have at least one poster of Mary Lou prominently displayed on the wall. She's an idol for many young American gymnasts. Her name and the Olympics automatically go together, and each time we meet it's a thrill for me all over again. She's very sweet and upbeat, and her smile fills the room.

Meeting Nadia Comaneci was a great moment for me also. I first met her shortly after my family and I had moved to Houston. The whole Karolyi clan attended an exhibition gymnastics event at Rice University. When Nadia found out I spoke Romanian, we became instant friends. Later I read more about her career and her tremendous struggles for freedom. She's an incredible inspiration to me.

It would be fantastic if I could achieve the level of success those two athletes have had. But whether I become a "star" gymnast or simply derive satisfaction from doing my personal best, I'll be happy. What I really push for is just to be up near the top, to be in a position to win, and to be able to say that I did something new with gymnastics.

No matter what coaches or athletes or news reporters might say, it's impossible not to let your mind drift ahead to the next major competition. Especially in a year like 1996, when the Summer Olympics is on everyone's mind.

I can't hide the fact that I'm totally ecstatic about the chance to compete in this year's Olympics. I'm trying to take it one day at a time, one step at a time. In my room at home I keep a countdown that I started in August 1995 right after the U.S. Nationals. So if you ever wonder exactly how many days there are till the Olympics, just ask me! I'll know!

These days leading up to the ultimate competition are the days every athlete cherishes throughout her life. These are the days that lead to the culmination of years of hard work and dedication.

I think about when Nadia and Mary Lou made their Olympic dreams come true, and I hope that soon my Olympic dream will come true too. For me, though, just getting as far as qualifying for the team is satisfying.

The qualifying trials for the Olympics will be held right before the Games. This year I think Kerri Strug and I will be the only members of Karolyi's Gymnastics who will qualify for the team. The other members of the seven-girl team will come from gymnastics clubs all over the country. I'll probably know them already, from having seen them at meets recently. It'll be a great chance to renew friendships and possibly make new friends. Even though we're all from different clubs and have different coaches, once we're part of Team USA, we'll pull together and represent our country as best we can.

I do imagine myself filing out with my U.S. teammates—fellow gymnasts as well as competitors from all the other sports—during the opening ceremonies, seeing all the different, incredible athletes from around the world, knowing that I have the honor of representing the United States. I just can't wait. Sometimes I can already hear the crowd roaring as the first Olympics of my generation, and the last ones of this century, begin. I know it will be one of the best days of my life.

The only thing that would increase the thrill of participating in the 1996 Olympics would be to win a medal. Every athlete has this dream—a dream of competing, winning, and securing a place in Olympic history. But no matter what the outcome, I will always remember who I am, and how hard I've worked to get this far, and all the people who have helped me in so many ways.

Sometimes I look in my mirror and pretend that I'm Dominique Moceanu, Olympic champion. Then I look in the mirror and see Dominique Moceanu, my parents' daughter. That's good enough for me.

AFTERWORD:
Olympic Triumph

Dominique Moceanu struck gold at the 1996 Olympics in Atlanta! She and her six teammates—Amanda Borden, Amy Chow, Dominique Dawes, Shannon Miller, Jaycie Phelps, and Kerri Strug—dazzled the crowd and the judges with their powerhouse routines, capturing a *first-ever* U.S. women's gymnastics team gold medal. It was a momentous night for Dominique, whose Olympic dream came true. It was a momentous night for America. Now Dominique is poised to embrace all the new challenges that lie ahead, both in her future as a gymnast and in every other aspect of her life.

A Few of
My Favorite Things

Colors: Red, pink, black-and-white (definitely *not* brown)

Athletes (nongymnasts): Michael Jordan, Kristi Yamaguchi, Scott Hamilton, Kurt Browning, Andre Agassi

Actors: Jim Carrey, Brad Pitt, Steve Martin

Actresses: Sandra Bullock, Jennifer Aniston

TV shows: *Fresh Prince of Bel-Air, Friends*

TV soap opera: *Days of Our Lives*

Cars: BMW convertible, Ford Explorer (definitely *not* big, clunky cars)

Cereals: Apple Jacks, Rice Krispies, Corn Pops, Wheaties

Foods: Steak, chicken breasts, Mom's Romanian specialties (such as *gris*), feta cheese, spinach

Least favorite foods (in case you're wondering): Onions, garlic, mushrooms, liver, squid—*yuck* to all of them!

Drinks: Apple juice, nonalcoholic strawberry daiquiris

Thing I couldn't live without: Personal computer

Music: Country and western

Musicians: George Strait, Garth Brooks

Countries: Japan, Brazil

Animals: My pets: Mitzy, my cat, and our goldfish

Sister: Christina (natch!)

Jewelry: My lucky elephant necklace

Guide to Gymnastic Events and Scoring

Calling all gymnastics lovers!

The Olympics is the hottest news story around this summer, and if you're a gymnastics fan, you'll probably be glued to the TV when your favorite athletes compete.

But what makes one gymnast today's superstar and another yesterday's news?

It all comes down to scoring. A gymnast can work toward the Olympics her whole career, but one measly *hundredth of a point* can make or break her.

This guide lets you in on the secrets of Olympic judging. Once you know what to look for, you and your friends can try to predict how your personal favorites will do in competition. You can cheer at their triumphs and groan at their mistakes. And you can keep track of their overall scores. You can even try to forecast the final medalists!

First, a quick overview.

GUIDE TO GYMNASTIC EVENTS

THE EVENTS

Women gymnasts compete in four events: the vault, the uneven parallel bars, the balance beam, and the floor exercise. (Men compete in six events: the floor exercise, the pommel horse, the still rings, the vault, the parallel bars, and the horizontal bar.) Each event is scored basically the same, with judges looking for strength, coordination, precision, and grace.

SCORING

The judges start at 10.00 and work their way down, right? Wrong! The base score for each event is 9.40. For each error, the judges deduct fractions of a point. However, a gymnast can earn up to 0.60 in bonus points for performing very difficult skills. So the perfect score for a difficult routine would be 10.00, and a perfectly executed easier routine would score only 9.40. In 1976 Nadia Comaneci made headlines by becoming the first gymnast ever to score a perfect 10.00 in Olympic competition.

In each event, the gymnast is judged on her compulsory and optional exercises. For the compulsory exercise, all the gymnasts must perform the same routine, which was determined after the 1992 Olympics. (This year's games are the last Olympics to include compulsory exercises.) Gymnasts choose their own optional routines. In the vault only, the gymnast gets two tries at the optional exercise, with the higher score counting.

Then the six judges rate the gymnast, with the highest and lowest scores tossed out. The eight remaining scores (four from the compulsory and four from the optional) are averaged to arrive at the gymnast's final score in that event.

By keeping track of your favorite gymnast's scores, you can follow where she is in the ranking—and tell whether she has a shot at the gold medal!

Now let's take a quick look at the four events.

THE VAULT

The vaulting horse is four feet high, five feet long, and eleven inches wide. In the women's vault the horse is perpendicular to the runway. (In the men's vault it is parallel to the runway.) The runway is three feet wide and eighty-two feet long. Gymnasts have to run that far to build up speed!

The vault can be divided into several stages. First the gymnast explodes off the springboard, whipping her legs up over her head. Depending on the vault, the gymnast may do a half twist before hitting the horse. In the support stage, the gymnast pushes off the horse with her hands, sending her body in a high arc with a variety of twists and saltos. Finally the gymnast hits the mat with a crisp, "stuck" landing.

Things to look for: precision, height, strength, and distance. *Deductions:* Fractions will be deducted for sloppy form—unpointed toes, back too arched or not arched enough—as well as for larger errors, such as a faulty mount or a bad landing. Judges like landings to be clean and precise, without any little hops or steps.

THE UNEVEN BARS

At their bases, the bars are three feet apart. The upper bar is about eight feet from the ground, the lower bar about five feet. The height of each bar can be adjusted slightly to fit the gymnast.

The uneven bars are the perfect showcase for a gymnast's concentration, coordination, and courage. Routines usually start on the low bar and move to the high bar. Watch for big swings on the high bar, as well as twists, handstands, regrips, and sudden changes of direction. The gymnast must perform at least two release moves, completely letting go of both bars.

Judges favor routines that flow gracefully from one movement to the next and end in a strong dismount.

Things to look for: good form, crisp movements, difficult elements. *Bad signs:* slipping off the bar, incomplete or faulty moves, sloppy landings.

THE BALANCE BEAM

The balance beam is four inches wide, fifteen feet long, and four feet from the floor.

The gymnast on the beam uses acrobatic, gymnastic, and dance elements to create an exciting and harmonious routine. A performance should include several instances of at least two skills, such as a cartwheel into a back handspring, performed in a series. Required moves include two acrobatic flight elements; a turn on one leg of at least 360 degrees; a leap of great height and distance; and an element close to the beam, such as a split. A routine must last between seventy and ninety seconds.

Things to look for: changes in rhythm, a graceful blending of acrobatic and dance movements, and a strong dismount. Also, balance, grace, difficulty of skills. *No-no's:* falling off the beam (it happens!), wobbling, and not completing the required elements.

THE FLOOR EXERCISE

The floor exercise is performed on a padded carpet measuring forty feet by forty feet.

In the floor exercise, the gymnast combines the athleticism of acrobatic tumbling with the theatricality of dance and music. This is the only event set to music. The gymnast must perform at least four passes from corner to corner, covering all areas of the carpet. One acrobatic pass must contain at least two saltos. Look for all passes to include moves of great height, distance, and amplitude. A routine must last between seventy and ninety seconds. Judges reward routines whose elements flow into each other smoothly and mesh well with the music. The best gymnasts incorporate both creative dance moves and difficult acrobatic skills.

Things to look for: difficulty of skills, imaginative use of the floor space, precise movements, and creative dance moves. *Bummers:* poor form, stepping off the mat, faulty or incomplete moves.

Here's an overview of the three different categories of competition.

THE TEAM COMPETITION

The twelve top-ranked national teams in the world compete in the Olympics. Besides determining the medals for the team competition, the events are very important because they determine who will compete for individual medals later.

Each national team has seven gymnasts. In the team competition, all seven gymnasts perform all four events. For each team, the top five scores in each event are added up. The team that earns the most points wins.

After everyone has completed the team competition, the thirty-six gymnasts who earned the highest overall scores get to compete for the individual all-around title.

Finally, the eight highest-scoring gymnasts from the team competition in each event get to compete for medals in the individual competition for that event.

Whew!

THE INDIVIDUAL ALL-AROUND
COMPETITION

Each of the thirty-six overall highest-scoring gymnasts from the team all-around performs a compulsory and an optional routine on all four events. Whoever totals the most points wins. That's pretty simple, no?

INDIVIDUALS

Finally, the individual medals! This is what gets people's blood really pumping.

The eight highest-scoring gymnasts from the team competition in each event compete in the individual competition for that event. As in the team and individual all-around, each gymnast performs both a compulsory and an optional routine to determine her score.

And just when you thought you had a handle on everything . . .

RHYTHMIC GYMNASTICS

Since 1984 rhythmic gymnasts have competed for Olympic medals. Rhythmic gymnastics incorporates dance moves, music, and hand apparatuses to create a compelling and graceful performance. Acrobatic moves, such as aerials and handsprings, are not allowed.

The Events

Rhythmic gymnasts compete for medals in five individual events: the rope, the hoop, the ball, the clubs, and the ribbon. Individual all-around medals are also awarded.

In the group competition, teams of five gymnasts perform together in two routines. For the 1996 Olympics, teams will perform first with five hoops and then with three balls and two ribbons.

Scoring

Two panels of judges score rhythmic gymnasts. One panel judges the composition—what the gymnast does. The other panel judges execution—how well the gymnast does it.

That wraps it up! Enjoy the Olympics!

Basic Gymnastic Moves and Positions

Aerial: any gymnastic skill that is performed without the hands touching the floor, such as an aerial cartwheel or aerial walkover.

Back handspring: a back flip of the body onto both hands, with both legs following as a pair. The gymnast begins and ends in a standing position.

Back somersault: a backward roll on the floor or beam, with knees in the tucked position. (The aerial version of this move is called a back salto.)

Back walkover: a move made from a back-arch (or bridge) position, bringing one foot, then the other, down toward the front. Similar to a back handspring but using smoother, more controlled movements, with arms and legs moving one at a time rather than in pairs.

Cartwheel: an easy move, in which the hands are placed on the ground sideways, one after the other, with each leg following. Arms and legs should be straight.

Front handspring: a forward flip onto both hands, with both legs following as a pair. The gymnast begins and ends in a standing position.

Front hip pullover: a mount used on the uneven parallel bars. The body is supported on the hands, the hips resting on either bar. Usually combined with a hip circle.

Front pike somersault: a forward somersault in which the knees are kept straight.

Front or forward somersault: a forward body roll on the floor or beam, with knees in the tucked position. (The aerial form of this move is called a salto.)

Front split: a split in which one leg is forward, one back.

Front walkover: a move made from a front-split handstand position, bringing one foot, then the other, down toward the back. Similar to a front handspring but using smoother, more controlled movements, with arms and legs moving one at a time rather than in pairs.

Handstand: a move performed by supporting the body on both hands, with the arms straight and the body vertical.

Hip circle: a move made by circling either bar of the uneven parallel bars with the hips touching the bar. If the hips do not touch the bar, the move is called a clear hip circle.

Layout: extension of the body to its full length, usually during an aerial move.

Pike: any move in which the body is bent and the knees are kept straight.

Roundoff: similar to a cartwheel, but with a half-twist, and the legs standing together in a pair. The gymnast ends facing the direction she started from.

Salto: a somersault.

GYMNASTIC MOVES AND POSITIONS

Somi-and-a-half: another way of saying one and a half somersault.

Sticking: refers to a dismount or final move that is performed without taking additional steps.

Straddle: a position in which the gymnast's legs are far apart at each side.

Straddle split: a split with legs out at each side. This move is used in all four women's events.

Straddle swing: a swing movement on the uneven parallel bars in which the legs are extended at each side.

Swedish fall: a move in which a gymnast does a free-fall drop straight onto the ground, with hands shooting out at the last second.

Tuck: a move in which the knees are brought to the chest.

Yurchenko: a mount for the vault, in which the gymnast does a roundoff onto the springboard.

Relive the dramatic gold-medal-winning night of the U.S. women's gymnastics team. . . .

**AMANDA BORDEN ~ AMY CHOW
DOMINIQUE DAWES
SHANNON MILLER
DOMINIQUE MOCEANU
JAYCIE PHELPS ~ KERRI STRUG**

These are the seven young women who vaulted to Olympic glory by becoming the first U.S. gymnasts ever to win team gold. Now THE MAGNIFICENT SEVEN: THE AUTHORIZED STORY OF AMERICAN GOLD tells each gymnast's story, based on exclusive interviews. Find out how each gymnast felt on that dream-come-true Olympic night; how she got started in the sport; how she trained rigorously for years; and all about her coaches, her family, her post-Olympic plans, and much more.

Full-color photos, many from family albums, capture a wealth of personal moments—beginning with baby shots and continuing all the way to the 1996 Olympics.